Boo

Christmas Calamity

This book comes with extra-special Felicity Wishes for Isabel and Olivia Nettleton. With thanks to your father for believing in fairies.
Love Emma x

Emma Thomson's
felicity Wishes®

FELICITY WISHES
Felicity Wishes © 2000 Emma Thomson
Licensed by White Lion Publishing

Text and Illustrations © 2005 Emma Thomson

First published in Great Britain in 2005 by Hodder Children's Books

The right of Emma Thomson to be identified as the author and illustrator of this work has been asserted by her in accordance with the Copyright, Designs and Patents Act 1988.

1

A Catalogue record for this book is available from the British Library

ISBN 0 340 91132 8

Printed and bound in Great Britain by Bookmarque Ltd, Croydon, Surrey

The paper and board used in this paperback by Hodder Children's Books are natural recyclable products made from wood grown in sustainable forests. The manufacturing processes conform to the environmental regulations of the country of origin.

Hodder Children's Books
A division of Hodder Headline Ltd, 338 Euston Road, London NW1 3BH

Emma Thomson's

felicity Wishes®

Christmas Calamity

and other stories

Hodder
Children's
Books

A division of Hodder Headline Limited

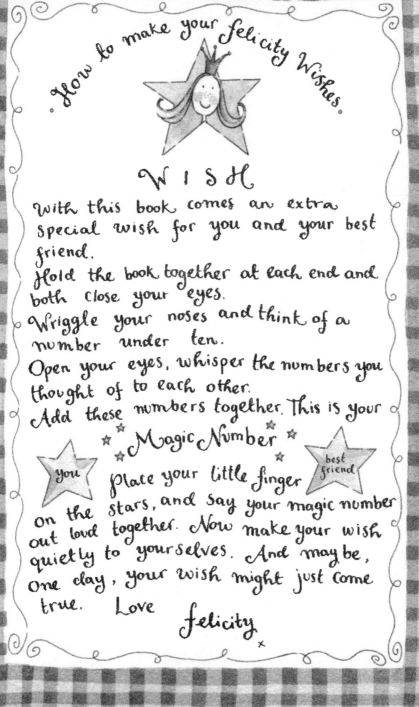

How to make your felicity Wishes

WISH

With this book comes an extra special wish for you and your best friend.

Hold the book together at each end and both close your eyes.

Wriggle your noses and think of a number under ten.

Open your eyes, whisper the numbers you thought of to each other.

Add these numbers together. This is your

Magic Number

you

best friend

Place your little finger on the stars, and say your magic number out loud together. Now make your wish quietly to yourselves. And may be, one day, your wish might just come true. Love

felicity
x

CONTENTS

Making Magic

Making Magic

Without knowing exactly why, Felicity Wishes found herself in a super-duper happy mood when she woke up on Monday morning. It all started when she put her slippers on the wrong feet and tripped up trying to get to the bathroom!

Instead of being annoyed she burst into a fit of giggles that stayed with her for the rest of the day.

* * *

"Heee heeee! Dooooon't!" squealed Polly, as Felicity tickled her wings from behind in the school playing field.

"You're in a good mood today, considering it's double Maths after assembly!" said Polly, bemused.

"I know," said Felicity, leaning her head back and balancing her wand on the end of her nose. "I'm not quite sure why I'm so happy – I just woke up like this."

"Me too!" said Daisy, fluttering over to join her friends. "I sang all the way in to school today. And when I had to fly straight back again because I'd

forgotten my packed lunch, I didn't
mind a bit."

"Everyone's happy today," sang
Holly, overhearing their conversation.
"Surely you've noticed!"
The four fairy friends looked at
each other and then turned to look
at their fellow classmates.
Almost all of them were beaming
great big smiles. If they weren't

telling jokes or pulling funny faces to amuse their friends, they were crumpled up in fits of giggles.

"It's as if someone's made a happy wish for everyone," Holly speculated.

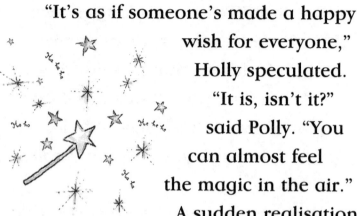

"It is, isn't it?" said Polly. "You can almost feel the magic in the air."

A sudden realisation struck Felicity and made her smile even more.

"Oh, of course, it's magic! It's Christmas magic!" she announced dramatically to the others. "I can't believe we'd all forgotten! Today is the first day of December and the countdown to the most magical day of the year begins right here."

Polly, Holly and Daisy squealed in unison.

"I've got an advent calendar at home that I've been looking at every day, dying to open it. I can't believe I forgot it this morning," said Daisy. "But then I suppose that's not *all* I forgot when I left for school!" she giggled, looking down at her packed lunch box.

"Oh, how exciting!" said Holly, who was in her element. When Holly graduated from the School of Nine Wishes she wanted to be a Christmas Fairy, and this time of year was her absolute favourite.

"And it's going to get even more exciting as each day passes," said Felicity, trying hard not to shriek. "Everyone knows that the magic of

Christmas just gets stronger and
stronger the closer we get to the
actual day!"

* * *

And that was exactly what happened.
As each day in December passed by,
Felicity Wishes and her fairy friends
felt Christmas magic spreading
everywhere. Music lessons were filled
with carol singing and bell ringing,

in Chemistry class they were taught
how to make tiny beautiful snow
crystals, and in Cookery class they
baked delicious
Christmas treats!

Even normal
household
chores like
cleaning
were full
of festive fun!

* * *

"There's so much
to do!" said Polly,
scanning her Christmas to-do list as
she and her friends relaxed with a hot
chocolate in Sparkles, the café on the
corner. "And I want to do it all at the
same time!"

Holly, Daisy and Felicity leaned over

towards Polly's chair so they could see what she had written.

"Polly, you're always so well prepared!" said Felicity, in awe of her friend's organisational skills. "I don't even have a list."

"But if you did have a list," said Polly, "what would be at the top?"

Xmas to-do list

Make Christmas cards

Collect holly and mistletoe

Get presents

Make treats

Choose tree

Get party outfit

Decorate tree

Roast chestnuts

Bake mince pies

Make Xmas cake

Felicity thought hard for less than a second before bursting out, "Presents, presents, presents! For all my friends!"

Holly sighed and shook her head in despair. "You've got your Christmas priorities all wrong," she muttered.

"A perfect Christmas outfit to make sure you shimmer at every festive party has to be number one!"

"Well, I'll tell you what has gone straight to the top of my list today," said Daisy, pulling out a large red envelope from her school bag. "Christmas cards! I've had my first one already!"

"Oh goodness, yes!" agreed Felicity. "If we don't send them soon, then everyone will think we've forgotten to write them."

"Or worse still, that we don't like them enough to send them a card," said Holly, grinning mischievously.

"Good point," said Polly, who really didn't want to offend anyone, especially at Christmas. "Well then, that's settled," she added, folding her list quickly and tucking it into her bag. "I'll see you all later – I'm off to make some Christmas cards!"

* * *

The next morning, Fairy Godmother had put up a special Christmas postbox in the entrance hall, as she did every year. It would be emptied every day for the cards to be given out in registration class before assembly.

Polly was a little later than her usual prompt self. The weight of all the Christmas cards she had made so carefully the previous evening had put a strain on her usual wing power.

Felicity bumped into her just as she began posting the enormous pile through the special school postbox.

"I can give you yours now if you like," said Polly, excitedly sifting through dozens of glittering envelopes.

Felicity clapped her hands. "No! No! Post it! Getting Christmas cards in registration class is much more exciting than being given them by hand. The more cards the better!"

Felicity Wishes was one of the friendliest fairies in the whole of the School of Nine Wishes and she was eager to see how many friends had remembered her with a card this Christmas.

* * *

"I only got one card," grumbled Felicity to Holly, Polly and Daisy when they met up at breaktime. She was a little disappointed, even though she hadn't sent any to anyone else yet.

"I've had five!" said Holly, pulling out the healthy pile from her bag and fanning them out for her friends to see.

"I've had three!" beamed Daisy,

carefully holding the envelopes to her chest.

"Well, I've had none!" said Polly unhappily. "It was *so* embarrassing. I sent fifty-three cards this morning and, in return, I didn't get a single one! Everyone in class got more than me."

"Well," said Felicity thoughtfully, "Christmas is about giving and not receiving. Knowing that you put smiles on the faces of fifty-three fairies is surely better than receiving a thousand cards!"

* * *

As the week went on, each of the fairy friends' houses gradually filled with glittery Christmas cards of all shapes and sizes. There were star-shaped cards, heart-shaped cards and even wing-shaped cards! And there was glitter everywhere!

Although she knew that it was tactless to boast about how many cards she had received, Holly couldn't help mentioning that she was going to have to fly down to Fairy Stationers to buy yet more ribbon to hang all her cards.

"I'll get you some," said Felicity helpfully. "I've got to go there myself later to get some more paper and glitter to make some extra cards. Every day I get another card from someone I'd forgotten and have to make them a card in return!"

"Thanks, Felicity," said Holly. "Now I have time to go and thank everyone for their lovely cards. I must be the most popular fairy in the school," she said, swishing her hair dramatically.

* * *

"I'm afraid we've no more ribbon left," said the shop assistant over the top of her glasses. "We've got another order due in early next week. It looks as though it's been a record year for

Christmas cards, and fairies everywhere are running out of places to hang them."

"Oh dear," said Felicity, thinking of Holly. "And I think I'm just about to add to the problem even more!" she joked, as she put down all her card-making materials on the counter.

As the fairy assistant carefully wrapped the materials, a beautiful handmade Christmas card caught the corner of Felicity's eye.

"Wow! Is this yours?" she asked, admiring the card.

"I wish!" smiled the assistant, picking it up carefully for Felicity to see properly. "I've promised to look for a special envelope for it while the young fairy that made it gets a stamp from the post office. Oh... here she is now!"

A very tiny fairy, with the smallest wand Felicity had ever seen, floated gently into the shop.

"I was just admiring your card!" said Felicity, beaming. "I've never seen anything as beautiful. There's so much detail and the glitter seems to be made with a thousand different colours."

The tiny fairy said nothing but nodded shyly and blushed gratefully as she made her way on tiptoes towards the counter.

"I'd love to make something like that for all my friends, but I'm afraid I don't have the skill, or the time," continued Felicity to the tiny fairy.

"I'd like to make more," said the fairy so quietly that Felicity could barely hear her. "But I don't have any friends to make them for."

"No friends?" asked Felicity, slightly taken aback.

"Well," said the tiny fairy, fluttering up to reach her card on the top of the counter. "I'm so little that everyone seems to forget I exist, especially at Christmas. I even have a small name, Mia, which no one ever remembers. I only got one card in the school postbox and that was from Fairy Godmother."

"I wouldn't worry, I only got one

card on the first day the postbox
went up too, and the
next day I got
nineteen!
You'll get
more before the
term ends, I'm sure."

"Oh no," said Mia. Felicity leant in
closely to hear what she was saying.
"I didn't mean just one card today, I
meant one card in total. And I'm not
expecting any more. Last year I got
none."

Felicity looked awkward. She
wanted to say it didn't matter, but
she knew how upset she had been
when she had received just one card.
Getting cards at Christmas-time came
with more than seasonal wishes, they
were written with love that let you

know you were in other people's thoughts and hearts.

"Why don't you come round to my house?" asked Felicity. "We could make some cards together. I've got too many to do, and you did say you'd like to make some more."

For a shy fairy, Mia suddenly became much louder. "Really?" she said, as she spun around smiling broadly. "I've got so many ideas, and lots and lots of magical things to use to make cards even more beautiful than this one. Are you sure you don't mind?"

"Mind?" said Felicity, amazed. "I'd love it! Come on, let's go!"

* * *

With the magic of Christmas surrounding them, Felicity and Mia flew to her house where they settled down to make cards. They stuck glitter, cut out snowflakes, folded patterned papers and dusted gold and silver sequins on an array of cards that quite literally shimmered with magic. Proud of their handiwork, they made special stickers for the back. "Made with Christmas magic by Felicity and Mia."

"I don't know which one to send to who!" said Felicity, admiring their hard work. "A part of me doesn't want to give any of them away – they are all so lovely!"

"The first one I am going to write is for you!" Mia said, picking out the biggest and most beautiful of all the cards for her new fairy friend.

"Well then, the first one I am going to write is for you too!" said Felicity, choosing the second biggest and most beautiful card.

* * *

The next day, after registration, the whole school was talking about the beautiful handmade cards they had received from Felicity and Mia.

"Thanks, Felicity," said Holly, flying up to her at break-time.

"I got the fabulous handmade card you and Mia made. I feel terrible; I completely forgot to send Mia a card. She's so tiny it's easy to miss her out. I'll make sure I send her one tomorrow."

And Holly wasn't the only one who had been prompted to remember Mia by the magical handmade cards. Fairies everywhere suddenly remembered the tiny fairy existed. Even Polly, who thought she'd sent cards to everyone in the school, realised there was one fairy she had missed out.

✳ ✳ ✳

The next day at school, Felicity jumped when someone suddenly gave her the most enormous hug from behind.

"Mia!" she squealed, spinning round and nearly knocking her over.

"Look what I got in registration this morning!" Mia beamed, showing Felicity a bag full of Christmas cards.

"Christmas magic works every time!" announced Felicity with a wink.

Winter Winner

Winter Winner

Felicity Wishes and Polly squinted into the darkness. The boiler room in the School of Nine Wishes was usually out of bounds, but Fairy Godmother had asked for a couple of volunteers to go down and find her special Christmas outfit and take it to Fresh and Bright, the fairy dry-cleaners on Star Street.

Every Christmas, on the last day of term, Fairy Godmother dressed up in an amazing red velvet cape with a

white fur trim. Beneath it, she wore a
stunning, sparkling, sequinned red
dress with the same soft fur trim as
the cape. And to top it all, Fairy
Godmother had a crown, taller and
more majestic than
any of her usual
crowns, with tiny
fur baubles that
jingled with
Christmas
magic.

Felicity and Polly held their breath. They loved adventures and the boiler room tingled with excitement. Even before they'd found the light switch, they saw the glitter of Fairy Godmother's Christmas outfit twinkling amongst the racks and shelves.

"WOW!" whispered Felicity to Polly as she turned on the lights and was dazzled by the glow from the corner. "There must be dozens of special outfits here, for every occasion imaginable."

"I never knew Fairy Godmother loved dressing up this much," said Polly, admiring rows upon rows of sparkling outfits.

"If every fairy in the school knew about this place then they'd never want to be anywhere else!" said Felicity, realising now why this room was normally out of bounds.

Felicity began to squeeze her way between piles of boxes towards the clothes rail on the far wall – which wasn't as easy as she'd hoped. There were large wicker hampers, enormous brown packing boxes and intriguing shoe boxes everywhere, each with a label showing its magical contents.

Distracted by the magnificent outfits, Felicity suddenly tripped and, as she tumbled, she brought with her an avalanche of boxes!

"Felicity! Are you OK?" shouted Polly, struggling to make her way through.

"Where am I?" asked a slightly

dazed Felicity, staring up at
something that looked like a cow! "I
think I must have hit my head – I can
see a cow!"

"It is a cow," said Polly, trying hard
to stifle her giggles. "It's a
pantomime cow!"

As Felicity carefully pushed the cow out of the way and looked around her, she realised she was quite literally up to her crown in costumes! Outfits and props for almost all the plays and pantomimes the School of Nine Wishes had ever performed surrounded her.

The long curly wig of an "ugly sister'" tickled her cheek as she pulled herself to her feet, only to find she had her foot in a beautiful glass slipper.

"Cinderella!" she sighed, remembering the school's magical production a few years ago. There was nothing like the festive fun of a pantomime to make you feel like Christmas really had arrived. And suddenly, Felicity had a fantastic idea...

✳ ✳ ✳

"Do you have to leave now?" moaned Holly, the next day, as Felicity got up to put her coat on.

"Yes!" said Felicity, reluctantly looking up at the clock. "Fairy Godmother's Christmas outfit will be ready to collect from the dry-cleaner's at four-thirty p.m. and I don't want to be late."

Felicity, Holly, Polly and Daisy were in Sparkles, the café on the corner, talking about their Christmas plans.

"Well, hurry back," urged Polly. "We need to work out something different to do, to bring everyone together at school this Christmas."

"I thought we'd agreed on another 'Hunt the Mince Pie' party," said Holly.

"After last time?" giggled Daisy, remembering the smell that had lingered for months in Maths class because the mince pie hidden down the back of the radiator hadn't been found!

"Well," said Felicity mysteriously, "you never know, I might just fly back with news of something more fun than Christmas crumbs!" And with a wink and a smile she was gone.

✳ ✳ ✳

Felicity Wishes felt nervous asking Fairy Godmother such an enormous favour at such a busy time of year. Fairy Godmother already had the Christmas carol concert, the Christmas fair and the Christmas school party

IMPORTANT NOTICE

Volunteers needed to help at the Christmas fair and to set up the hall for the Christmas party.

Room 6 at lunch-time

to organise. Surely she wouldn't want to organise a Christmas pantomime too?

"Felicity! What a fabulous idea! It will make the most wonderful secret surprise," Fairy Godmother said, clapping her hands together with

glee. "But I'm afraid I'm far too busy to organise it this year."

Felicity's wings drooped with disappointment. "Oh well, never mind," she said as she started to make her way towards the door.

"However, someone else could organise it," said Fairy Godmother with a knowing smile.

"But who?" asked Felicity, racking her brains for a suitable person.

"You, silly!" said Fairy Godmother, smiling.

Felicity beamed. She knew the magic of Christmas was really working now. It was the best present Fairy Godmother could have given her!

* * *

When Felicity returned to Sparkles she couldn't contain herself any longer.

"Fairy Godmother has given me permission to organise a school pantomime with all my friends!"

"A pantomime?" said Holly, Polly and Daisy, a little surprised. It was not the ecstatic reaction Felicity had been expecting.

"Yes! Yes!" said Felicity, making tiny fairy jumps as she spoke. "It's going to be a wonderful secret surprise for the rest of the school!"

Polly was Felicity's most sensible friend, and whilst she loved her exciting and impulsive nature, Polly knew that Felicity's ideas weren't always the most practical.

"That sounds great!" said Polly, tentatively. "As long as we can practise over the Christmas break – then we will be ready for the performance in January."

"No, silly!" said Felicity, confidently. "I've arranged with Fairy Godmother for us to show it to the whole school on the last day of term, as a secret surprise!"

Daisy didn't need to check her diary; she already knew there were only ten school-days left until the end of term.

"Do you think that's enough time?" she asked, already knowing the answer.

"Bags of time!" said Felicity, who had confidence enough for all of them.

"Nonsense!" said Holly, the only fairy friend brave enough to speak up. "It won't work. We don't even have scripts."

"But we do!" said Felicity, proudly

pulling a large folder
with the word
"Cinderella" on the
front from her bag.

"OK, well, we don't have
any props or costumes!" challenged
Holly.

"But we do!" said Felicity, waving
the keys to the boiler room. "Come
on, I'll show you!"

The fairy friends put on their
winter coats, picked up their
bags and flew with Felicity to the
School of Nine Wishes.

* * *

When Holly and Daisy saw the
magical contents of the boiler room,
their doubts about the pantomime
quickly fluttered away.

"There's no choice!" said Holly,

picking up a dazzling golden ball-
gown and holding it against herself.
"We have to get this pantomime
ready in time. It wouldn't be a proper
Christmas without it!"

All the fairy friends nodded excitedly as they started to rummage through the boxes of treats.

* * *

Over the next few days, all the friends could eat, sleep or think about was the Cinderella pantomime. The tricky part was trying to keep it secret from the rest of the school. Instead of their days being filled with all the usual Christmas preparations, like choosing a tree and making decorations, the four fairy friends were busy learning lines and getting into character to make the pantomime surprise extra-special. But to some fairies it was becoming a little too obvious…

"Felicity Wishes! These mince pies are dreadful," said Miss Butterpuff, the Cookery teacher, as she looked

at the burnt remnants
on Felicity's table.

"Sorry, Miss
Butterpuff,"
said Felicity
absent-mindedly.

"I'll make some more. And then after
that I'll sweep the hearth, wash the
floor and sleep by the fireplace
in these old grey rags."

Miss Butterpuff and the rest of the class looked puzzled.

"Felicity! What on earth do you mean?" she boomed. "You are wearing your favourite pink dress today, not an old grey rag! And we don't have a hearth or a fireplace here."

Suddenly Felicity snapped out of her daydream. She was so happy Holly, Polly and Daisy had agreed she could play the part of Cinderella in the pantomime that she had completed immersed herself in the role, even in class!

* * *

Holly had had an equally disastrous time in her Games lesson. Playing the part of one of the ugly sisters meant that she had to practise being mean

and selfish. Only, when she refused to
let anyone else play with the ball in
hockey and was asked to leave the
pitch, she found it hard to explain
her actions.

"Sorry, Miss Skipping," she said,
head bowed, "I don't know what
came over me."

"Well I should think not! It's as if you were someone else!" said the Games teacher. "Such selfishness, especially at Christmas-time, has no place on this team."

"Yes, Miss Skipping," said Holly, trying not to smile. Secretly, she was very happy that she'd managed to act selfish so convincingly!

* * *

When the fairy friends met up after school in the entrance hall, Holly and Felicity discovered that Daisy and Polly had had an equally awkward time.

"Fairy Godmother let us leave our last lesson early," said Polly, surprisingly unhappy. "She wanted us to check whether we had enough seats for everyone in the school

62

before she made the
announcement about
the pantomime."

"That's great!" said
Felicity, who had
actually forgotten
all about the seating arrangements.

"Not so great when every time you
get the chairs out to count them, the
cleaners tidy them away!" said Polly,
exasperated.

"And we couldn't tell them to leave
the chairs out because it's a secret!"
said Daisy, nearly pulling her hair
out with frustration!

The friends were finding it harder
and harder not to let their secret out.

* * *

As the last day of term drew near,
Felicity and her friends rehearsed

morning, noon and night! They were utterly exhausted and not feeling nearly as festive as they usually did at this time of year.

"I don't know if I can do this any more," pleaded Daisy, collapsing on a settee. "Even though it was a lovely idea to make everyone else's Christmas extra-special this year, it feels like we're missing out on our own."

Holly nodded. "Last night everyone went carol singing, but I had to stay in and learn my lines."

"I'm afraid I have to agree," said Polly. "I'm normally so organised at Christmas but, so far this year, I've only got cards ticked off my list."

Felicity felt dreadful. "I know we've all given up a lot to put on this pantomime, but there's only two more days to go," she said, desperately trying to convince her friends.

"We all know our lines perfectly and have just finished adding the final touches to our beautiful costumes... it seems a shame to give up now when we're so close to doing something so magical. And you have to admit that even though it's been hard work, it's been fun too."

Polly nodded. "Oh it's definitely been fun!" she said, giggling. "I love that bit when Holly's pulling funny faces behind Daisy and only the audience can see."

"Oh! And that bit where Holly's bloomers fall down at the start of the second half!" said Daisy, laughing.

"Perhaps we are being a bit hasty," said Holly, realising how much attention she would forfeit by not performing.

"Hmmm," said Polly, thinking seriously. "There's still a week to go between breaking up from school and Christmas Day, which is plenty of time to do all our own Christmassy things."

Daisy nodded. "I'm happy to carry on with the pantomime, if everyone else is!"

"On with the show it is, then!" said Felicity, beaming and hugging all her friends.

* * *

The last day of term arrived quickly. Expectations about the forthcoming holiday had reached fever pitch and fairies everywhere were in a state of frenzied excitement.

Fairy Godmother looked as magical as

Christmas itself in her
beautiful red velvet
outfit. And as a
special treat, she
allowed everyone
to wear whatever
they liked
on the last day and
bring in their favourite
games to play. But none
of the fairies suspected
that Fairy
Godmother
also had another
special treat, in
which she would
play the starring role.

* * *

"You may be wondering why I have
called you all away from your lessons

to take your seats in the school hall," said Fairy Godmother loudly, across the sea of fairy faces.

"Christmas is a time for giving and receiving. Each of you, I know, has given this Christmas-time already; in the presents you have made carefully and the cards you have sent. Now it is your time to receive. Four very special fairies and I would like to present you with an extra-special end-of-term Christmas surprise... a Cinderella pantomime!"

And suddenly the heavy stage curtains swished open to reveal a set that took everyone's breath away. Excited whispers and gasps filled the hall as Felicity, Holly, Polly and Daisy walked on stage, dressed in their beautiful outfits.

"I told you it would be worth it!" said Felicity breathlessly, as she bounced back in to the wings after what she thought was their final encore.

"They're calling for us again!" squealed Polly, listening to the loud cheers of "more" above the applause.

"I know we've just given but it feels like we've received, too," said Holly, beaming a broad smile.

"Then you've all felt the true fairy magic of Christmas!" said Fairy Godmother as she led the fairies out on stage, hand in hand, for another encore.

"This really is the best Christmas ever!" shouted Felicity to her friends above the cheers.

The magic of Christmas
has worked

when giving and receiving
feel as good as
each other

Christmas Calamity

Christmas Calamity

Term-time at the School of Nine
Wishes was at an end and Christmas
magic was in the air. As a final treat
before they broke up, Felicity Wishes
and her three friends, Holly, Polly
and Daisy, had performed Cinderella
in front of the whole school to
rapturous applause. But the biggest
encore had been for Fairy Godmother,
who had made a guest appearance
as... the Fairy Godmother!

"Fairies, that was wonderful," said

Fairy Godmother emotionally. "The perfect end to a perfect school year."

"Thank you," said Felicity and her friends, as they watched the hall empty of fairies.

"It was so much fun," said Polly, still beaming with delight.

"Right, there's just the cleaning up to do and then you can all go home," said Fairy Godmother, looking round at all the props and costumes. "It shouldn't take you too long. I've put some large boxes back stage for you and arranged with the caretakers to store them."

The fairies' wings drooped. They were dying to join their friends to celebrate the end of term and were now regretting the promise they had made to put everything away after the pantomime.

Slowly, the fairies started to tidy up. Holly packed away the ugly sister costumes, Felicity made sure her own Cinderella outfits were folded neatly in a box, Daisy began to dismantle the backdrops and Polly carefully stored away the props.

"Do you know the first thing I'm going to do when we've finished here?" called Polly from the rafters.

"Choose a Christmas tree?" guessed Daisy. "Because that's what I'm going to do!"

"Nope," shouted Polly.

"Go to Top Fairy and get a dress for the Fairy Christmas Eve Ball?" called Holly, who was going to do what was most important to her.

"Make yummy Christmas presents for all your friends?" shouted Felicity, who was planning to do the same.

"No to all of those!" said Polly, flying down to join them. "The first thing I'm going to do when we've tidied up here is..." she paused dramatically, "...make a snow fairy! LOOK! It's snowing!"

Felicity, Holly and Polly spun round quickly and ran to the window.

"It really is snowing!" said Felicity,

so excited her crown nearly pinged off.

"I can't believe it!" said Daisy, clapping her hands.

"And it's settling!" squealed Holly,

more excited about the opportunity to wear her new furry boots than anything.

"Oh, let's go out and play in the snow now," said Daisy excitedly. "It might have melted by the time we finish up here."

"Good idea!" said Felicity. "It is *so* beautiful when it snows!"

Holly and Polly didn't need any convincing. They had already abandoned their jobs and were pulling on their winter coats.

"Last one to get hit by a snowball wins!" said Felicity, flying at top speed out of the doors.

* * *

Having snow at Christmas was an extra-special treat, because there hadn't been any snow in Little

Blossoming for years. It wasn't long
before the fairies were covered in it!

"Look at me," shouted Felicity,
sitting in a snow chair she'd made.
"Who needs to go to Sparkles for a

hot chocolate when I have all the refreshment I need right here!" And she tipped back her head, opened her mouth and let a dozen snowflakes tumble from the sky straight into it.

"Snowflakes are too beautiful to eat," squealed Daisy, running over to Felicity and showing her the collection she had gathered on the back of her mitten. "Every single one is different, you know," she said in awe.

The fairies played for hours in the snow until the sun started to disappear over the hilltop.

"We should go in now," said Polly, who was just putting the finishing touches to her snow fairy. "It's getting late and we've still got to finish packing up."

"I hope the snow is still here tomorrow," said Holly, shivering a little.

"Me too," said Felicity, getting up and dusting herself down. "If it is, we could go sledging in the morning!"

"And ice-skating on the pond in the afternoon," said Daisy, leading the way up the front steps back to the school hall.

"Perfect!" they all chorused.

"Just like today," said Felicity, looking back at the amazing snow sculptures they had made.

* * *

By the time the fairy friends had tidied everything away, the sun had well and truly set. They had joked and gossiped for much longer than any of them had realised and when Polly looked at the time it was almost seven o'clock.

"Before we leave, I'll just go and tell the caretakers that the boxes are ready to collect," said Polly, putting on her coat. "If you turn out the lights, I'll meet you all by the front doors."

"I saw the caretakers in the Science lab when we came in from playing in the snow," called out Felicity.

"That was ages ago!" shouted Polly, as she fluttered up the main staircase. "They could be anywhere in the school now."

* * *

The school was eerie at night,

especially when all the lights were off. Large shadows loomed on bare walls and the tiniest noise made a sinister echo. Felicity, Holly and Daisy huddled together, waiting for Polly to return.

"What was that?" squealed Felicity.

The three fairy friends jumped with fright as they heard a large bang.

"Me slamming the door, silly!" said Polly, as she appeared behind them. "There's no sign of the caretakers so I think we should just go, and leave everything here for them to tidy away tomorrow."

Anxious to get out in the snow again, the fairies readily agreed and headed straight for the front door.

"It's stuck," said Felicity, tugging on the door.

"What do you mean, stuck?" squealed Holly.

"Let me have a go," said Polly. "It's probably just a bit stiff from the cold."

"It's locked!" said Daisy, who had got down on her knees and was peering through the gap between the doors.

"It can't be," said Holly, starting to panic.

"It is!" squealed Felicity.

"But we can't be locked in. I've got a million and one things to do at home before Christmas Day," stammered Holly dramatically, echoing everyone's secret fears.

Xmas to-do list

Make Christmas cards ✓
Collect holly and mistletoe
Get presents
Make treats
Choose tree
Get party outfit
Decorate tree
Roast chestnuts
Bake mince pies
Make Xmas cake

"No, you're right. We can't be locked in over Christmas, Holly, but we might just be locked in overnight," said Felicity, trying to calm her friend. "I'm sure the caretakers will remember that they haven't put the boxes away and will be back first thing tomorrow."

"The most important thing is to make the best of a bad situation for tonight," said Polly, thinking positively.

Holly was unconvinced.

"Come on," urged Felicity, finding
a light switch and turning it on.
"It's an adventure. The whole school
to ourselves! We can go to all those
places that are usually out of bounds."

"The staff room!" said Daisy,
clapping her hands with glee. "I've
always wanted to know what it's like
in there."

* * *

And together the four fairy friends
flew anywhere and everywhere, each
secretly hoping to find the caretakers,
or spot an unlocked door or window
to the outside world that would allow
them to go home. But none of them
found anything.

"Hey!" shouted Holly down the

hallway to the others. "I've found the perfect place for us to sleep tonight." She opened the door to the sick bay.

"Great idea! But let's have some supper first in the canteen – I'm starving," called out Polly.

"Isn't it a bit naughty taking food that doesn't belong to us?" asked Felicity, a little concerned.

"I'm sure Fairy Godmother would understand," said Polly, reassuringly. "She wouldn't expect us to be stuck in here all night and not eat."

Felicity's tummy rumbled in agreement.

✳ ✳ ✳

That night was more fun than any sleepover the fairy friends had ever had before. They had midnight feasts in the canteen, made up dance

routines on the assembly stage, told spooky stories in the library and fell sound asleep in the cosy beds in the sick bay.

No one woke up the next morning, for one important reason. There was no daylight. Unbeknown to the sleeping fairies, snow had fallen heavily all night and covered the whole of Little Blossoming in a deep, thick blanket of snow.

Everyone was stuck inside their homes except those, like Fairy Godmother, who lived on the hill. The only part of the School of Nine Wishes left visible was the top of the flag-pole, which peeped out of a mountain of snow.

"What time is it?" mumbled Polly, slowly waking up. "It feels like I've had a lie-in, but it's dark enough to be midnight."

"It's midday!" exclaimed Felicity, turning on the light and looking at her watch. "I'll open the curtains and let some light in."

"I hope we haven't missed the caretakers!" said Holly, as she sat up and rubbed her eyes.

Suddenly Felicity gave a sharp intake of breath. "I don't think the caretakers will be going anywhere today. In fact, I don't think anyone will be going anywhere today!" And she stood back to allow her fairy friends to see the view outside the window.

"Is that snow?" asked Daisy, who thought she was still dreaming.

"Yup!" said Felicity, excitedly.

"We're snowed in! And if we're snowed in, so is everyone else!"

"Only, everyone else won't have a store cupboard the size of the canteen!" said Daisy, hearing her tummy rumble.

"Or a whole room of games to play with," joined in Polly.

"Isn't it funny? Yesterday we were unhappy to be stuck in here, but now I'm really pleased to be having such an adventure," said Felicity to the others.

Holly wasn't as eager to agree. "Felicity, you're forgetting one thing. It *would* be lucky to be stuck here if we'd done all the Christmassy things we wanted to, but none of us have pulled a single christmas cracker this year, made a single present, or even decorated a Christmas tree."

Felicity thought hard, which was a difficult task for her when she'd just woken up. She didn't like to see her friends unhappy and knew there must be something she could do to make it all right.

"Everyone stay here," she said. "I'm going to bring you all breakfast in bed. The magic of Christmas works in mysterious ways. All we have to do is believe."

With that Felicity flew out of the door and down to the canteen.

* * *

When Felicity returned it wasn't only the breakfast she had made.

"Taa daaa!" she sang as she burst through the door with an enormous cheese plant. "I know it's not strictly

a Christmas tree, but with these
homemade decorations and a little
sparkledust from the
Science lab, it
looks just as
beautiful."

Holly, Polly and Daisy rolled on the floor with laughter.

"Where on earth did you find it?" said Holly, trying hard not to spill her tea as she fought off another flurry of giggles.

"Fairy Godmother's office," said Felicity, handing out warm buttered toast. "Anyway, that's not all I found. There was a book in the library called *Magical Presents to Make and Bake at Christmas*, and I found all these Christmas CDs in the music room. This is going to be a great Christmas!"

And for the first time since they'd been snowed in, the fairy friends felt the magic of the festive season fill their hearts.

＊ ＊ ＊

At last, the night before Christmas arrived. Holly had created special party outfits for them all in the Sewing room. Polly had made Christmas snacks and hot spiced juice to  have at their fairy party. Felicity had created a brand new Christmas dance routine to Suzi Sparkles' latest track and Daisy had made beautiful decorations in the art room to hang everywhere.

 The school hall looked
magical.

"Oh look!" said Daisy,
pointing out of the top
window in the hall
as she pinned up
the last decoration.
"Fireworks!"

"You know,"
said Felicity, flying
up to her friend, "I'd almost forgotten
Little Blossoming existed."

"If there are fireworks, then the
snow must be melting and fairies are
able to leave their houses," said Holly,
excitedly as she joined them.

"Has anyone tried to open the front
door today?" shouted up Polly from
the ground.

"No!" said Felicity. "I've been having

such a good time, I'd forgotten all about it."

Polly fluttered quickly out of the room and headed towards the front door.

"I'm not sure I'd like to go, even if we could," said Holly, looking at the beautiful decorations in the hall.

"Me neither!" said Daisy. "This has been so much fun!"

"That's lucky!" shouted Polly, fluttering back into the room. "Because we are still snowed in and, I just realised, even if the snow had melted, we would still be locked in!"

"Of course! We need Fairy Godmother or the caretakers to unlock the school before we can go home," said Felicity, not even trying to hide her delight. "It looks like we are here for Christmas, then!"

"Hooray!" Holly, Polly and Daisy cheered.

* * *

The fairies were just about to make another round of hot spiced juice when they heard a noise from outside.

"There's someone out there!" cried Daisy, pointing out of the window.

"There can't be. The snow still goes up to the top of the window!" said Holly, unconvinced.

"There is! There is! Come and see," squealed Daisy excitedly.

The fairies heard a small tinkle, followed by an enormous crash. Suddenly, the entire entrance hall was flooded with snow as the front doors to the school flew open.

"Fairy Godmother!" squealed Felicity, Holly, Polly and Daisy at once, not quite believing their eyes.

Fairy Godmother dusted herself down and flew towards the fairy friends. "You're safe!" she said, hugging each of them in turn.

"They're safe!" she boomed loudly up the gaping snow tunnel behind her.

Muffled cheers and hoorays got louder as, one by one, dozens of fairies emerged out of the snow and into the entrance hall. Soon the room was filled with every fairy in the school.

"We've been tunnelling for days," said Fairy Godmother, walking into the school hall and gasping at the beautiful transformation. "And it looks like we got here just in time for a party!"

"With all our friends here, this really is going to be the most magical Christmas ever!" said Felicity, feeling a warm glow spread from her nose to her toes.

Emma Thomson's
felicity Wishes®

Felicity Wishes and her
friends go on a holiday of
a lifetime to visit Felicity's
new penfriend in

Enchanted Escape

Perfect Penfriend

Felicity Wishes had spent hours hunting for her special pink pen but she still couldn't find it anywhere.

"Borrow mine," said Polly in a hushed voice, as they were studying in the library.

"But it's not pink!" whispered Felicity.

"Does that matter?" asked Polly, frowning.

Miss Page, the library monitor, glared in their direction and put her finger to her lips. "Shhhhhhh!"

Yes, it does matter, wrote Felicity on a scrap of paper and handed it to her friend.

"Why?" Polly scribbled back.

Felicity wiggled a beautiful sheet of sparkling pink paper in front of her friend's nose.

I need to write a special letter, wrote Felicity, looking round to check that Miss Page wasn't watching them any more.

Polly suddenly stifled a squeal. Felicity's favourite pink pen was nestled neatly behind her ear! She tweaked it out and passed it to her friend, leaning over her shoulder to see who she was writing to.

Felicity was scribbling a response to an advert in *Fairy Girl* magazine. It read:

Pen Friend Needed:

Friendly fairy would like true friend to share dreams. My hobbies are knitting, cloud-trekking and singing whatever comes into my head.

Please reply to: Beatrice, The Cottage, Rainbow Wood, P M 12

* * *

Being the friendliest fairy in Little Blossoming, Felicity had found Beatrice's appeal hard to ignore. By the end of lunchtime she'd written a four-page response, telling Beatrice all about herself, her best friends, the School of Nine Wishes, and her favourite flavoured ice cream.

"It's very good!" said Polly, after Felicity had shown the letter to her friends during break-time.

"Are you sure it's OK?" asked

Felicity. "You don't think it's too over the top?"

"No, honestly!" assured Holly. "It's wonderful!"

"I would love to get a letter from you," said Daisy. "Your letters are so magical."

Felicity skipped happily to the nearest postbox and made an extra-special wish just for Bea before posting her letter.

* * *

Every day Felicity watched for the Post Fairy before she left for the School of Nine Wishes, and it wasn't long before a large yellow envelope landed on her doormat in a cloud of glitter.

"Isn't it great!" said Felicity excitedly to her friends when she finally arrived at school. "Bea's written four whole pages, on both sides too!"

Felicity's friends gathered round her, flapping their wings with excitement, as Felicity read out loud her very first penfriend letter.

"Gosh, it's so exotic!" said Holly, admiring the beautiful paper. "They don't sell writing paper like this at the Fairy Stationers in Little Blossoming!"

"And her handwriting is so lovely! Do you think she writes like that naturally or do you think all fairies where she lives write like that?" pondered Polly.

"And look at the delicate flower she's attached to the letter. I've never seen anything as pretty as this ever. I wonder what it is?" asked Daisy.

Felicity picked up her fluffy pink

pen straight away. "I'll write back to Bea and find out the answers to all your questions. I have a few questions myself – I want to know more about her friends, they sound so lovely!"

✷ ✷ ✷

Over the next few weeks, Felicity and Bea exchanged letters almost every other day. Felicity couldn't believe they had so much in common!

Dear Beatrice

My best friend is Polly – she's good at everything and often has her head in books, studying to be a tooth fairy. Then there are my other two friends, Holly and Daisy. You'd love them. Holly is the queen of fashion in Little Blossoming and always looks stunning. Daisy is a real dreamer and loves spending time in her garden, chatting to her flowers. What are your friends like?

Write soon.
        Love Felicity x

A few days later, Beatrice's reply dropped on Felicity's doormat. She flew downstairs as fast as her wings would take her and opened her letter straight away.

Dear Felicity,

Oh my goodness! Your friends sound fabulous and just like my friends! My best friend is Amber and she won first prize for the best smile competition this year. My other friend, Star, dreams of setting up her own fashion label one day, and Jasmine is green-fingered and works part-time at the local garden centre. I can't believe how similar they are!

Write soon.

Lots of love, Bea. x x

After reading Bea's letter, Felicity suddenly had an idea! "Wouldn't it be wonderful if I met Bea, Polly met

Amber, Daisy met Jasmine and Holly met Star!' she thought, smiling to herself. "I am sure we would all get on really well and half-term is coming up so we could visit them then."

Quickly Felicity grabbed her pen and immediately set about writing back to Bea to share her big idea with her...

Read the rest of

Emma Thomson's
felicity Wishes®
Enchanted Escape

to find out all about

Felicity's big idea.

If you enjoyed this book, why not try another of these fantastic story collections?

Clutter Clean-out

Designer Drama

Newspaper Nerves

Star Surprise

Emma Thomson's
felicity Wishes

Enchanted Escape
and other stories

Enchanted Escape

Emma Thomson's
felicity Wishes

friends forever
and other stories

Friends Forever

Emma Thomson's
felicity Wishes

Sensational Secrets
and other stories

Sensational Secrets

Emma Thomson's
felicity Wishes

Whispering Wishes
and other stories

Whispering Wishes

Happy Hobbies

Party Pickle

Wand Wishes

Christmas Calamity

Dancing Dreams

Spooky Sleepover

Fashion Fiasco

Also available in the Felicity Wishes range:

Felicity Wishes: Secrets and Surprises

Felicity Wishes is planning her birthday party, but it seems none of her friends can come. Will Felicity end up celebrating her birthday alone?

Felicity Wishes: Snowflakes and Sparkledust

It is time for spring to arrive in Little Blossoming, but there is a problem and winter is staying put. Can Felicity Wishes get the seasons back on track?

Felicity Wishes: Mix-ups and Magic

Felicity Wishes' fairy friends are terribly down in the dumps. Without realising it, Felicity makes a wish for each of her unhappy friends, but Felicity's wishes are a little mixed-up...

Felicity Wishes: Friendship and Fairyschool

It is nearly the end of school for Felicity Wishes, and all her friends know exactly what kind of fairies they want to be – but poor Felicity does not have a clue!

The World of Felicity Wishes

Felicity Wishes' world is full of wonderful, sparkly things. Friends that make her giggle, fashion that makes her tingle and a million other yummy things that she can't wait to share with you.

In this stunning novelty book, you can discover Felicity's secret hiding places, meet her best friends and learn the Fairy Dance routine. You can also find out what type of fairy you could be!

Felicity Wishes shows you how to create your own sparkling style, throw a fairy sleepover party and make magical treats in this fabulous mini series. With top tips, magic recipes, fairy products and shimmery secrets.

Sleepover Magic

Cooking Magic

Fashion Magic

Hair Magic

Make-up Magic

Beauty Magic